LAURA VICKERS

ILLUSTRATED BY PEGGY WARGELIN

Flying to See Janet

A Fun Guide to the Airport Experience

Jessica Kingsley *Publishers*
London and Philadelphia

of related interest

Frog's Breathtaking Speech
How Children (and Frogs) Can Use the Breath to
Deal with Anxiety, Anger and Tension
Michael Chissick
Illustrated by Sarah Peacock
ISBN 978 1 84819 091 7
eISBN 978 0 85701 074 2

Deeno's Dream Journeys in the Big Blue Bubble
A Relaxation Programme to Help Children Manage their Emotions
Julia Langensiepen
Illustrated by Gerry Turley
ISBN 978 1 84905 039 5
eISBN 978 0 85700 201 3

The Red Beast
Controlling Anger in Children with Asperger's Syndrome
K.I. Al-Ghani
Illustrated by Haitham Al-Ghani
ISBN 978 1 84310 943 3
eISBN 978 1 84642 848 7

For Janet, who we love just the way she is.

And for the rest of us, who are all more joyous
when we know what the heck is going on!

First published in 2012
by Jessica Kingsley Publishers
116 Pentonville Road
London N1 9JB, UK
and
400 Market Street, Suite 400
Philadelphia, PA 19106, USA

www.jkp.com

Library of Congress Cataloging in Publication Data
A CIP catalog record for this book is available from the Library of Congress

British Library Cataloguing in Publication Data
A CIP catalogue record for this book is available from the British Library

ISBN 978 1 84905 913 8
eISBN 978 0 85700 656 1

Printed and bound in India

Contents

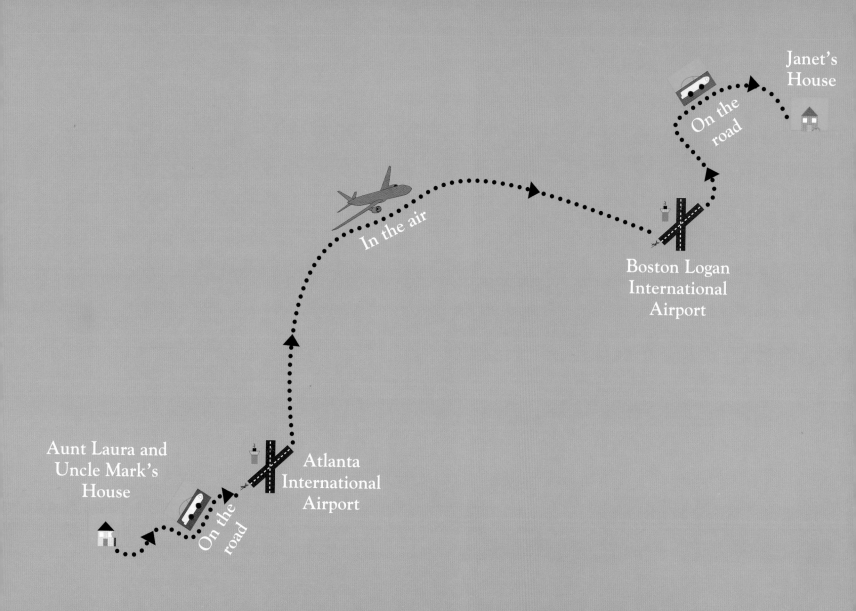

Packing and getting ready can be stressful, but that is normal. Everyone wants to be sure they have everything they need. You also want to be sure you arrive at the airport on time.

If the airport is far from your house, you may need to stop on the way there. You can get gas for the car, grab a snack, just stretch your legs, or take care of anything else you need to.

I have to pee!

Ooo! McDonald's!!

I'll bet Uncle Mark needs to pee!

Atlanta Airport 25 Miles

You have to be careful not to get too big a drink, or you may need to stop again really soon!

Bye!

Every airport is different. You have to find the things you like in each place. One of the things we like at the Atlanta airport is the Park and Ride that takes you from the parking lot to the terminal where the planes are. Your car gets to rest just where you parked it until you return. Be sure to remember its location in the parking lot!

After you get to the terminal, you "check in" to let the airline know you're there. That's where you give luggage which is too big to fit near you in the plane (or any you just don't want to carry) to the airline. They put a tag with an ID number on each bag, and give you a ticket with the same number so you can prove it's yours when you pick it up. Then it rides on a conveyor belt to be put in the cargo section of the plane, below where the passengers sit.

After check in, you move on into the airport. We love the moving sidewalks in the long hallways. Uncle Mark likes to race Aunt Laura. This is more of a challenge when Aunt Laura walks on the moving sidewalk and Uncle Mark does not.

Some airports have art to look at. At the Atlanta airport there is some neat African art we like.

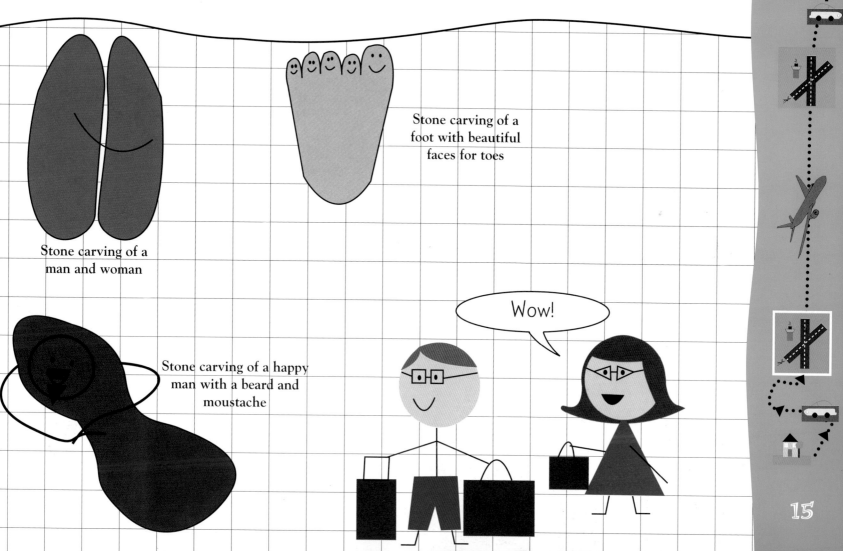

Stone carving of a foot with beautiful faces for toes

Stone carving of a man and woman

Stone carving of a happy man with a beard and moustache

Wow!

No matter which airport you fly out of or into, you always have to go through security. The job of the security people is to keep everyone safe.

Going through security can be fun, especially if you are really prepared. First they check to make sure you have a ticket. Then, if you have a picture ID they see that you are really you by checking that you look like your picture.

SECURITY

Good thing I had my picture identification and ticket ready!

Yes! That i you! Please move forwar

Next, they make sure no one is carrying anything unsafe onto the plane.
Even though you might think of a very funny joke about security, it's important not to say it out loud because someone might think you are serious.

Then they scan you, to make sure you aren't carrying any metal objects.

Sometimes the alarm goes off, but don't be alarmed (ha ha!). Someone just forgot to take off their watch or keys or something and put it in the tray. If something more exciting than that happens, please remember to tell me all about it!

X-Ray Machine

BEEP!
BEEP!
BEEP!

Step back.

That would never happen to us!

Oops! This never happens to me!

In some big airports, there is a special type of scanner that you stand in for a few seconds instead of just walking through. Sometimes the machine can't see as well as it needs to, so a person will gently pat your clothes. Don't worry. The security people will let you know what to do if you get confused, and the adult travelling with you will always be there.

There are lots of cool looking stores in airports, but most items are very expensive. Don't be surprised if no one wants to buy anything. Sometimes Uncle Mark and I buy something anyway.

ICE CREAM

That was $10.00!

What?!

Yum!

It's important that everyone is at the gate when the plane is ready, so it can leave on time. They have a waiting area for each flight. There are rest rooms and water fountains all around the airport which you can use if you need to wait a long time. There is usually a big window so you can look at the planes getting ready.

Getting onto the plane is the most boring part. It is like standing in the lunch line at school, only you don't get anything to eat when you're done.

Uncle Mark always puts the luggage in the overhead bins. Then we put our small bags under the seat in front of us. It can feel crowded, but it is exciting to see the wide variety of people who are going to the same place you are!

Where you sit can be exciting, too. All seats have something good about them. I like to sit where I can see the wing of the plane, but I also like to just see sky! I can see out of the plane a little even when I don't have a window seat, and being on the aisle can make it easy to stretch and move even though I can't see as well.

Sometimes there are interesting things to see inside the plane, too!

Odd hair to look at:

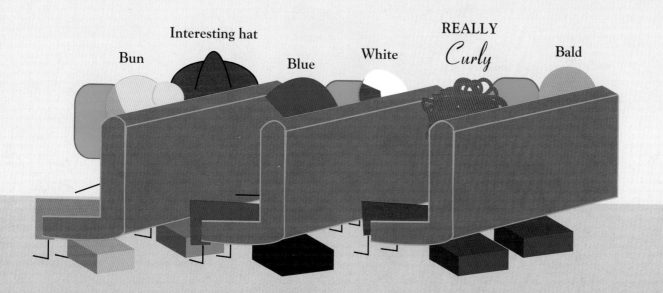

Bun   Interesting hat   Blue   White   REALLY *Curly*   Bald

After you're seated, the flight attendants give a safety talk. It's good to know there is a plan in case there are any problems. One of the most important parts of the talk is that you must always wear your seat belt when the "Fasten Seat Belt" sign is on.

Usually there is an announcement to tell you when you have to turn off your games, phone, internet, and other electronic devices for a short time during take off, and another one when it's safe to turn them back on. This will happen again during the landing.

Uncle Mark's favorite part of flying is the take off. I find take off to be a little noisy. If you forget the noise and don't look out the window it is just like riding a school bus though. Uncle Mark says the reason why planes can fly is very scientific. It has to do with air pressure and stuff. I just think it's cool!

Sometimes my ears can feel funny during take off and landing, and even for a while after. I chew gum or yawn a lot to get them back to normal. It won't last more than a few hours, even if you don't do the yawning and chewing.

After the plane has leveled off, I look forward to the flight attendants bringing everyone a snack and a drink. Sometimes I get a cola. Uncle Mark always gets water and some crackers.

One annoying thing is when the captain makes announcements that are too loud or too quiet. Most of the time, though, the announcements are just right.

That was loud! Oh well, it didn't last long.

What did he say? Must not have been important.

Thanks for that information!

When I want something to do, I check my "Go Bag." I pack things to do and things for "just in case" times. Travel sometimes has bad smells, so if we know a bad smell is coming we may just tough it out. If it's strong or lasts a long time we keep cinnamon gum for Uncle Mark to chew and perfume for me to put on a tissue and hold up to my nose.

What might belong in your "Go Bag"? What do you like to do when you are bored on board? (Ha ha!) What flavors and smells do you like? Maybe you want to have a plan for your "just in case" times, too.

No flight is ever the same, so it's fun to fly many times.
Over the years I have experienced a lot.

Beautiful sunset

City lights
twinkling at night

Perfect blue sky with
puffy white clouds

Thunderclouds and
lightning with rain

Water with tiny, white waves
and itty, bitty boats

Flying through a cloud
(Of course, fog is just a cloud
on the ground)

Whoa!

Fun! I feel like I am on a school bus traveling on a bumpy dirt road.

Bounce!
Bounce!
BOUNCE!

Turbulence or "chop"

There isn't always turbulence, but there was some on my last flight. I placed my pen on the pad, and you can see what happened.

Going to the bathroom

Sometimes there is a line to go to the bathroom, or the "Fasten Seat Belt" sign is on, so you need to wait patiently. It's a good idea to go before you get on the plane if you have time.

This is such a cute little bathroom!

When we get bored, we read or fall asleep. Other things you can do are look out the window, daydream, look at magazines they may have on the plane, or choose from the "Go Bag." The snack tables can come in handy! Sometimes on long flights they even have a movie.

ZZZZZZ...

When I get tired of sitting, I secretly exercise my butt muscles. Nobody knows but me!

I wonder if anyone else ever does this?

Right cheek!
Left cheek!
Right cheek!
Left cheek!
Hold together!

Right cheek!
Left cheek!
Right cheek!
Left cheek!

My favorite part is the landing. Before the plane lands, it flies lower so there is often more to see. At some point the landing gear comes down. You can hear all sorts of cool mechanical sounds, and if you are able to see the wing you can watch its flaps raising and lowering as the pilot prepares to land. No two landings are exactly alike.

Sometimes if a pilot makes a good landing people on the plane will applaud. They are showing appreciation for the pilot's skill.

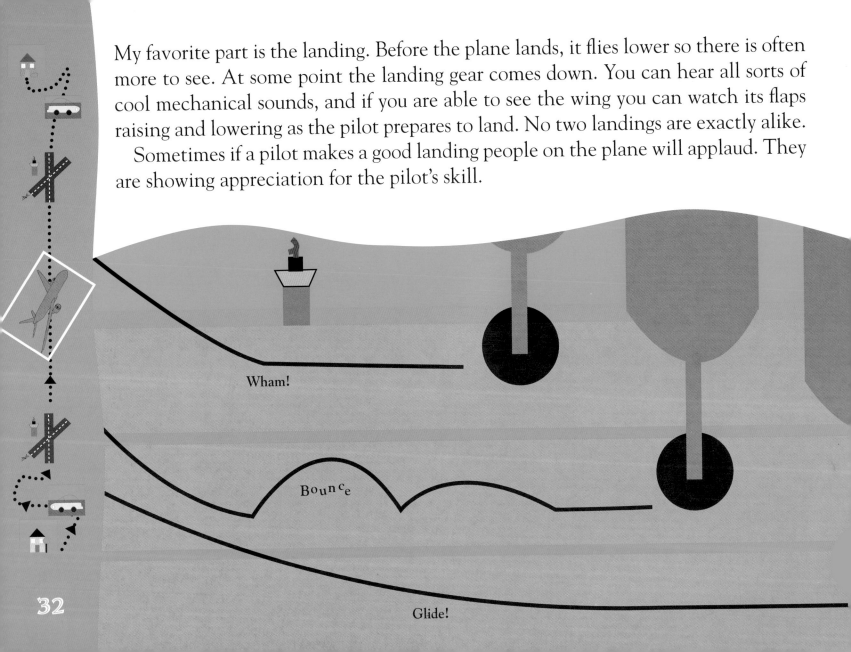

Wham!

Bounce

Glide!

Getting off the plane is the opposite of getting on. Usually the people at the front get off when the door opens, and then you get off in order of your seat number. It's a bit faster than getting on, since it's so orderly.

If you gave some of your luggage to the airline before you got on the plane, you have to go to "baggage claim." It's fun to see your luggage taking a ride on the big belt. If you're meeting someone at the airport, sometimes they find you at baggage claim and sometimes you meet them after you get your luggage.

Flight	From	Claim
AA4563	Atlanta	2
UA3374	Frankfurt	6
BA65	London	3

Of course, the best part of flying is getting to see the ones you love when you get there!

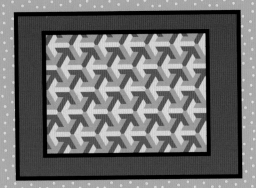

When you get to fly someday, be sure to tell me all about your trip. Maybe you can even write a book about it!

My Flight By Janet

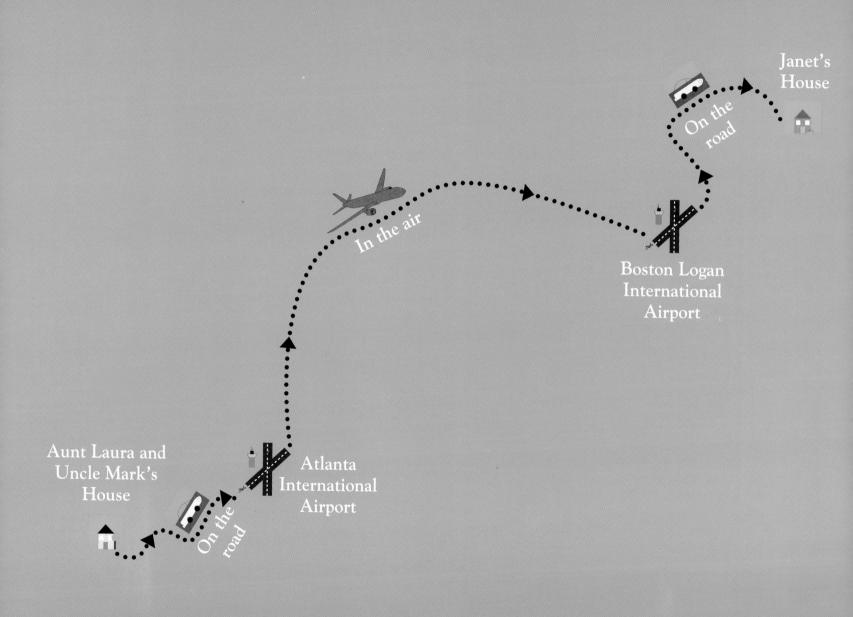

Janet's House

On the road

Boston Logan International Airport

In the air

Aunt Laura and Uncle Mark's House

On the road

Atlanta International Airport

Suggestions for parents

Dear Parents,

This book started as my sister Laura's hand-drawn notes on a lined paper notebook when she wrote a funny chronicle of her trip from Boston to Atlanta for my daughter Janet. It was so helpful for her that when I had to make a book in a graphic design class I chose to base it on Laura's story as my way of trying to help other parents. I hope you find the additional suggestions below useful as well.

Take care,

Peggy Wargelin

GETTING TO, AROUND, AND FROM THE AIRPORT

Try to visit the airports ahead of time, or have someone else do so:

- How will you get there? If in a car, where will you park? If with a friend, in a taxi, public transport, etc., what will that be like and where will you be dropped off?

- Can you find a map of the airport? Which terminal(s) does your airline fly from and are there any neat spaces your child might like? Boston airport has spots with kinetic sculptures that Janet finds fascinating. Detroit airport has a tunnel between terminals with a rainbow light show and relaxing music that you watch as you ride on the moving walkways. Many airports have fountains.

A calming, quiet place with something interesting to see may be worth some extra time at the airport to visit.

- What food is available in that terminal? Different terminals may have different restaurants. Which, if any, chain restaurants are there that you could try away from the airport beforehand to find something your child likes to eat?

- How do you get around in the airport? Most have moving sidewalks, elevators, and escalators, but some also have buses and monorail/subway trains. This may be a challenge or entertainment, depending on your child.

- Bring two adults if you can, for as much of the trip as possible. One can attend to the child and the other can:

  o scout for places to sit, eat, etc.

  o handle paperwork at check in, security, boarding, and baggage claim

  o clean things before the child gets there.

SECURITY

- Avoid wearing anything that will trip the detectors. Women, do NOT wear an underwire bra. Once you have made it through the scanner, you aren't allowed to come back. I was stopped at a scanner, and was then required to go to a second, different one.

Because I had sent my child through first, she couldn't come back to me, even though I had to go to the other scanner!

- The United States Transportation Security Administration (www.tsa.gov) has a page devoted to traveling with children with disabilities. It has a comforting statement that "at no time during the screening process will you be separated from your child," but as demonstrated by the "underwire scenario" above, things may differ in practice. Knowing what is supposed to happen may help if something comes up on your trip.

- If you have two adults, send one through with all the bags. When you can see the first is ready, send the child through, and then the second adult goes through.

- Be sure to read and understand the regulations for what is allowed in carry-on luggage in your area and for your flight ahead of time. Completely empty water bottles and water-filled toys before going through security, and refill them afterwards.

- There are exceptions to the security rules for medications, infant formula, or anything medically necessary, but you must present each item separately to security personnel. For Janet's nut allergy, we carry an Epipen® with the full prescription label on it, and a note from her pediatrician stating that it is medically necessary for her to have it with her. You can probably get a therapeutic item through security with a doctor's note stating it is medically necessary. We once had Play-Doh® confiscated because it looked like plastic explosives, but we had no note.

PLANNING FOR SENSORY ISSUES

If possible, have the child help make the plan for dealing with sensory issues and choose what they'd like to bring in the "Go Bag." If Janet feels she has something she can do in a situation, it gives her a sense of control that reduces her anxiety.

Noise

Especially in places with high ceilings and lots of people, for example check-in and security, there can be a lot of echoing background noise. Noise reduction headphones or listening to music from headphones can help. Ear plugs come in many different styles; you may be able to find one your child likes. Bathrooms can be noisy, especially with the loud, unexpected flushes. Carts used by the airline to transport people emit a loud, piercing beeping as a warning.

Crowds

If your child is feeling overwhelmed and needs more space in a crowd, we have found it useful to use our adult arms and bodies combined with the luggage to create at least a small breathing space around Janet. She doesn't like to be touched when stressed, so we can't just pick her up to raise above the crowd.

Smells

Strong smells can happen anywhere, especially in crowded places. As discussed in the book, bringing something with a strong flavor to chew or a favorite perfume or smell to put on a tissue to hold to the child's nose can help. Places to be especially aware of are drop off/pickup areas (where exhaust builds up) and bathrooms. Also, if it is a warm day, be aware that an aircraft has limited electricity from the time it pushes back from the gate until just before take off; there may be several minutes without air conditioning.

Temperature/Touch

You can bring a first aid chemical cold pack and use it to cool down your child if they become too hot. A battery powered mini-fan can also be useful in the heat. If it is cold, don't count on a blanket or pillow to be provided on the plane. Bring lots of layers, and perhaps chemical warming packs. If your child likes to touch everything, or has allergies like Janet, bring some antibacterial wipes and wipe everything the child might touch.

ON THE PLANE

When booking, make sure you get the seat type your child needs (window/aisle/center). Many people will trade seats on the plane if you need them to, but don't count on it. Seats near the back can have very loud, constant engine noise. Seats near the bathroom can feel crowded as people stand in line. If the window is over the wing or engine, you may not be able to see any scenery.

Sometimes the airline will change the plane type after you buy the ticket. What was a great seat in the middle of the plane may now be in the back, or what was a window seat may now be a center seat. We usually aim for near the front (but not *at* the front) on the left side; seat "A" remains a window seat, no matter what.

Ask for (and watch for the start of) early boarding. Many people board early even if they don't need to so, to make sure you really are "early," stand at the front of the line as soon as it looks like they are getting ready to announce. Don't wait until they actually do.

In addition to smell, another potential bathroom issue may be the loud (scary) noise of the toilet and sink water being sucked out when you flush it. You may want to flush the toilet for your child after they leave the bathroom. Be aware the sink also drains noisily, by suction.

Bring gum or something to chew to help with ear pain as the pressure changes. Motion sickness medicine might be a good precaution.

If the child reads the emergency card or is distressed by the safety briefing, try to explain the "just in case" aspect of it and then distract them.

IN GENERAL

Bring food your child likes. Don't plan on food being available. On one of our trips there had been a trucking strike and the restaurants had no supplies. You might be delayed on the plane before take off or diverted to a different airport. Better safe than sorry.

Bring lots and lots of things your child might like to do—some new, and some familiar and comforting; some to do with you and many to do alone. We found that a laptop with lots of games loaded and a WiFi connection to get online worked well. The laptop can be used to show DVDs. We also brought a Nintendo DS with many spare games. It was a special treat for Janet to have basically unlimited electronic game time. It was nice for us, since bringing extra games didn't require extra weight or space. Don't forget the charging cords and/or extra batteries. Sensory toys are also good, as are drawing supplies, stickers, puzzle books, a portable CD player, etc.

Gook luck. The first time is always a challenge, but good preparation makes it a lot easier. Janet now loves to fly. We hope your child will, too!